Published by Scholastic Inc.
90 Old Sherman Turnpike, Danbury, Connecticut 06816.

For information regarding permission, write to:
Disney Licensed Publishing
114 Fifth Avenue, New York, New York 10011.

ISBN 0-7172-6822-5
Designed and produced by Bill SMITH STUDIO.

Printed in the U.S.A.
First printing, June 2004

DISNEY
PRINCESS

Chip's New Friend

A Story About
Compassion

by Jacqueline A. Ball
illustrated by
Duendes del Sur

SCHOLASTIC INC.

New York   Toronto   London   Auckland   Sydney
Mexico City   New Delhi   Hong Kong   Buenos Aires

On a shelf in the kitchen of the Beast's castle, where the enchanted teacups slept, Chip was still awake. He was thinking about tomorrow and how he wouldn't have anyone to play with.

"*I*t will be the same as today," he thought sadly. "Everyone will be too busy to play with me."

*T*hat day, like so many others, Chip had wandered around asking everyone, "Will you play with me?"

Belle had read him a story, but then the Beast had needed to talk to her.

Chip's mother had sung him a song, but then she had to cook supper. Even Chip's teacup brothers and sisters were busy, being filled with tea and then washed and dried later.

After a while, Cogsworth and Lumiere also became too busy to play.

"*I*f only I had someone to play with me all the time," Chip thought, as he fell asleep that night.

At breakfast the next morning, Chip looked so sad that Belle suggested they go out to the barn and see her horse, Phillipe.

"Okay," said Chip, brightening up.

"Take your scarf," Mrs. Potts reminded him. "It's cold outside."

*I*n the chilly barn, they placed sweet-smelling hay in Phillipe's stall. They gave him buckets of oats and fresh water. And Belle replaced his horse blanket with a new one.

Just as they were ready to leave, they heard a tiny squeak coming from a wooden cart.

Chip bounced over to investigate. "Look, Belle! It's a mouse!"

A tiny mouse sat in the cart, shaking from the end of his tail to the tip of his pink nose.

"Why is he shaking?" Chip asked.

"The poor thing is cold," Belle answered.

"He's probably frightened, too."

Belle felt sorry for the small creature. Tenderly,
she tried to warm him in her gloved hands.

"*I* bet he would feel better if we gave him something to eat," suggested Chip.

"I think you're right," said Belle. "Let's take him into the castle."

*T*hat whole afternoon, Chip and Belle took care of the mouse. Chip gave him tea from his very own cup. Chip also fed the mouse pieces of cheese.

Chip and Belle made a mouse-sized bed out of hay. Then Chip's mother let him use fabric scraps from her sewing basket to make a blanket.

Chip named the mouse Twinkles because his tiny eyes were so bright. After supper, Chip tucked Twinkles into his little bed and tiptoed away.

But the next day, the mouse bed was empty.
"Twinkles?" Chip called anxiously.

He heard a squeak—a loud, strong squeak that
sounded like a giggle.

Twinkles jumped out from behind a chair leg
and squeaked again. He felt better and wanted to
surprise Chip.

Chip was delighted. Finally, he had his very own, very special friend!

He and Twinkles played hide-and-seek . . .

. . . hopscotched across floors . . .

. . . and raced up and down the staircases.

Chip also taught Twinkles songs . . .

. . . and read him stories.
For days, the mouse
never left Chip's side.

*T*he two friends often had so much fun that they fell asleep snuggled together in the middle of the day.

"I don't think I've ever seen Chip happier," Mrs. Potts commented to Belle one morning.

"I'm so glad he has a playmate," said Belle.

Suddenly Chip burst into the room. "I can't find Twinkles!" Chip cried. "He's gone!"

Mrs. Potts, Belle, and Chip searched the castle, calling Twinkles's name and scattering pieces of cheese. The mouse was nowhere.

"What if he's sick again?" Chip asked.

"We'll find him, dear," Mrs. Potts said.

*I*n the kitchen, Belle noticed that the door
was open.

"The Beast must have left it like that when he
went to the barn this morning," said Mrs. Potts.

"Maybe Twinkles went outside," said Belle.

Belle and Chip put on warm clothes and searched the snow-covered gardens, but Twinkles wasn't there.

Then the Beast opened the barn door. "I see Twinkles inside!" Chip cried. "But there's another mouse with him!"

$\mathcal{T}$winkles was in front of Phillipe's stall. Next to him sat a bigger grey mouse.

"Twinkles!" Chip called. "Come on back to the castle with me!" Chip hooked his handle around his friend's tail and tugged gently. It was the game they enjoyed most.

*T*winkles slipped out of Chip's grasp and scampered away with the other mouse.

Chip was confused. "He doesn't want to play with me anymore," he said, trying not to cry. "He likes that other mouse better than me!"

*B*elle knew how sad and hurt Chip was feeling. Her heart ached for the little teacup. How could she help him feel better?

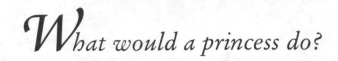

What would a princess do?

*B*elle carried Chip back to the castle. "I know how special Twinkles is to you," she said. "I can tell you're special to him, too. But different creatures have different ways. No matter how much Twinkles likes you, he still needs to be with other mice."

Chip frowned. "He's not my friend! I never want to see that mouse again!"

"Oh, Chip, you feel angry now because your feelings are hurt," Belle said gently. "But I know you'll understand when you've had some time to think about it."

*B*elle was right. By lunchtime, Chip was ready to visit Twinkles again. He wanted to make sure Twinkles was all right.

As soon as Belle and Chip went into the barn, Twinkles ran up to Chip and tickled him with his whiskers. Minutes later the other mouse joined them. He began to tickle Chip, too!

"*I*t looks as if you have *two* friends now," Belle exclaimed, feeling happy for Chip.

Chip and the mice played in the barn all afternoon. He didn't even notice when Belle quietly slipped away.

$\mathcal{M}$uch later, when Belle came back to tell
Chip that supper was ready, he was beaming.
"Two mice are even more fun than one," he said.
"Twice as nice," Belle agreed.

Chip was so tired from playing that he almost fell asleep at supper. But he was still beaming when Belle put him to bed.

"I'm lucky I have two special friends," he said sleepily. "I can play with them in the barn any time I want."

As Belle kissed Chip good night, she added, "And they're lucky to have an understanding friend like you, Chip—a friend with compassion."

The End